The Invisible Man

H.G. WELLS

SADDLEBACK
EDUCATIONAL PUBLISHING

Saddleback's *Illustrated Classics*™

SADDLEBACK
EDUCATIONAL PUBLISHING

Three Watson
Irvine, CA 92618-2767
Website: www.sdlback.com

ISBN-13: 978-1-56254-910-7
ISBN-10: 1-56254-910-3
eBook: 978-1-60291-154-3

Printed in China

12 11 10 09 08 9 8 7 6 5 4 3 2

Welcome to
Saddleback's *Illustrated Classics*™

We are proud to welcome you to Saddleback's *Illustrated Classics*™. Saddleback's *Illustrated Classics*™ was designed specifically for the classroom to introduce readers to many of the great classics in literature. Each text, written and adapted by teachers and researchers, has been edited using the Dale-Chall vocabulary system. In addition, much time and effort has been spent to ensure that these high-interest stories retain all of the excitement, intrigue, and adventure of the original books.

With these graphically *Illustrated Classics*™, you learn what happens in the story in a number of different ways. One way is by reading the words a character says. Another way is by looking at the drawings of the character. The artist can tell you what kind of person a character is and what he or she is thinking or feeling.

This series will help you to develop confidence and a sense of accomplishment as you finish each novel. The stories in Saddleback's *Illustrated Classics*™ are fun to read. And remember, fun motivates!

Overview

Everyone deserves to read the best literature our language has to offer. Saddleback's *Illustrated Classics*™ was designed to acquaint readers with the most famous stories from the world's greatest authors, while teaching essential skills. You will learn how to:

• Establish a purpose for reading
• Use prior knowledge
• Evaluate your reading
• Listen to the language as it is written
• Extend literary and language appreciation through discussion and
   writing activities

Reading is one of the most important skills you will ever learn. It provides the key to all kinds of information. By reading the *Illustrated Classics*™, you will develop confidence and the self-satisfaction that comes from accomplishment— a solid foundation for any reader.

Step-By-Step

The following is a simple guide to using and enjoying each of your *Illustrated Classics*™. To maximize your use of the learning activities provided, we suggest that you follow these steps:

1. *Listen!* We suggest that you listen to the read-along. (At this time, please ignore the beeps.) You will enjoy this wonderfully dramatized presentation.

2. *Pre-reading Activities.* After listening to the audio presentation, the pre-reading activities in the Activity Book prepare you for reading the story by setting the scene, introducing more difficult vocabulary words, and providing some short exercises.

3. *Reading Activities.* Now turn to the "While you are reading" portion of the Activity Book, which directs you to make a list of story-related facts. Read-along while listening to the audio presentation. (This time pay attention to the beeps, as they indicate when each page should be turned.)

4. *Post-reading Activities.* You have successfully read the story and listened to the audio presentation. Now answer the multiple-choice questions and other activities in the Activity Book.

Remember,

"Today's readers are tomorrow's leaders."

H. G. Wells

Herbert George Wells, an English novelist, historian, journalist, and author of science-fiction stories, was born in 1866. His father was a shopkeeper, and his mother worked occasionally as a housekeeper. After completing his early formal schooling, Wells worked as a teacher. He later received a scholarship to study at a school with a special focus on the sciences.

His training as a scientist is shown in his imaginative science-fiction stories. Wells described trips in airplanes and submarines when such modes of transportation had not yet been invented. *The Time Machine* describes a trip into the future, and *The War of the Worlds* is an account of an invasion from Mars. Several of his science fiction works have been the basis of popular movies.

Though he is best-known for his science fiction stories, Wells wrote a variety of other works. He was a strong believer in education and wrote three lengthy books in which he tried to bring important ideas in history and science to the general public. His numerous books, articles, and essays also show his bold support of social change.

H. G. Wells died in 1946.

Saddleback's *Illustrated Classics*™

The Invisible Man

H. G. WELLS

THE MAIN CHARACTERS

Thomas Marvel

Dr. Kemp

Mrs. Hall

The Invisible Man

Officer Jaffers

Would an Invisible Man rule the world? Could he steal great wealth as an unseen thief? Kill people who stood in his way? Scare the countryside and make people all obey him? That's what the young scientist, Griffin thought—until he found that being invisible caused great troubles and kept him from his evil wishes. His terrible actions only made the whole world his enemy, until he was hunted down like a mad dog.

One cold day in February, a stranger walked into the Coach and Horses Inn, in Iping Village....

A room... and a fire! Please! I'm frozen!

Right away, sir.

After the landlady lit fire in his room, she was surprised when....

Shall I take your coat and dry it, sir?

No, Mrs. Hall. I want to keep it on for now.

As you like, sir. The room will be warm soon.

Later, when Mrs. Hall brought a tray....

Your food, sir.

Oh! You surprised me.

He did not begin to eat, but held his napkin in front of his mouth as he spoke.

You may take those things to dry, Mrs. Hall.

Rather a strange man, he is....

The puzzled landlady talked to her kitchen maid....

The mystery grew and grew....

Later....

Sir! Would you mind if Mr. Teddy Henfrey fixes the clock in your room?

You came in again without knocking....

Heavens! Below his nose it looks like his mouth and chin are missing! Or is it my eyes?

Mrs. Hall, I should explain that I am a scientist, and I cannot have people coming in and bothering me while I work. Understand?

Yes, sir! Sorry, sir! Teddy won't take long.

Alone with the strange guest, the repairman was uneasy....

That wrapped-up man gets on my nerves!

You! Get your repairs done fast and get out.

Mr. Henfrey decided to stay longer, but....

It's a simple repair, and you're taking too long.

All right, I'm leaving!

Next day, as the boxes were brought.....

When the angry guest went outside to talk to the boss....

To everyone's surprise....

The landlady brought her husband to the door....

12

In the dark room without a lamp burning...

Sir, are you bleeding? ...heavens! Your coat sleeve-it has no hand at the end!

You fools!

Get out! I'm not hurt. Just have the rest of my bags brought in. Do you hear?

He's a wild man!

Alone....

There! New pants and a glove, and every inch of my body is covered again. Darn that dog! He nearly gave away my secret.

When the last box had been brought in....

He unpacked more bottles and jars than the drugstore has! And dumped all the straw on the floor. I guess I'll have to clean up.

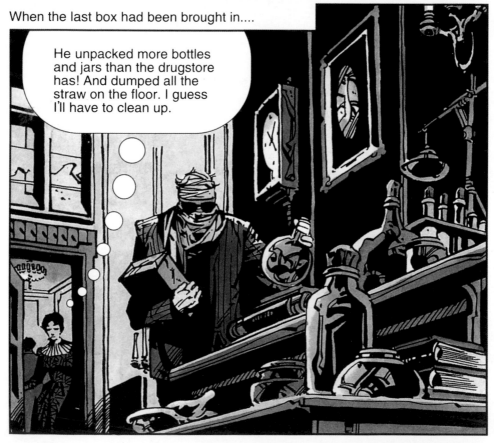

But Mrs. Hall saw something extraordinary....,

In the following days, the sound of bottles smashing and books being thrown about often came from the stranger's room....

Later, bringing tea and cleaning up....

He lost his temper every day,
as Mrs. Hall could not help hearing.

But sometimes at night, he
walked around the town....

Confound it! I have failed again!

He's always talking to himself as if he has a terrible problem. And he seldom leaves his room.

That's the mystery man from the Coach and Horses. He nearly ran us down as if he didn't see us at all!

Oh, mamma! It's the Bogey Man!

He certainly looks like it.

Meanwhile, throughout town, people had different ideas about the
bandaged mystery man.

Bet he's a crook hiding out from the police!

A murderer, that's what!

Naw! Just a harmless nut!

I say he practices black magic.

Young people, less frightened, made fun of the stranger.

One day Dr. Cuss, the town's doctor, decided to visit the mysterious stranger....

The doctor met the same shocking surprise Mr. Hall had.

I want to know why he is working with chemicals. Is he looking for a new cure?

An empty sleeve! No visible hand at all, beyond the cuff. Am I dreaming?

Empty sleeve, eh? No hand, eh?

Then what is squeezing your nose, my dear sir? Ha ha!

Ouch!

Out of my way! I'm going to see the minister about this!

The following Monday night, at the vicarage, the Reverend Bunting and his wife were suddenly awakened....

Early in the morning, at the Coach and Horses....

Even worse....

As the frightened pair fled....

They even wondered more later when....

Recovering from all these strange things, the landlady faced her guest, in the bar.

I don't care what strange things you do. You haven't paid this bill. You said you were expecting money.

I did, didn't I?

The guest took out his stolen money....

Here it is!

All right. But my nerves are going bad, and I have some questions to ask you, if you don't mind.

I want to know how you got in if your room was empty before? And why the chair lifted itself and came at me? And all the other strange things that have been going on. Answer me, sir!

Stamping his foot in great anger, the mystery man yelled back, and....

You dummies! You don't understand who or what I am. I'll show you, by heaven!

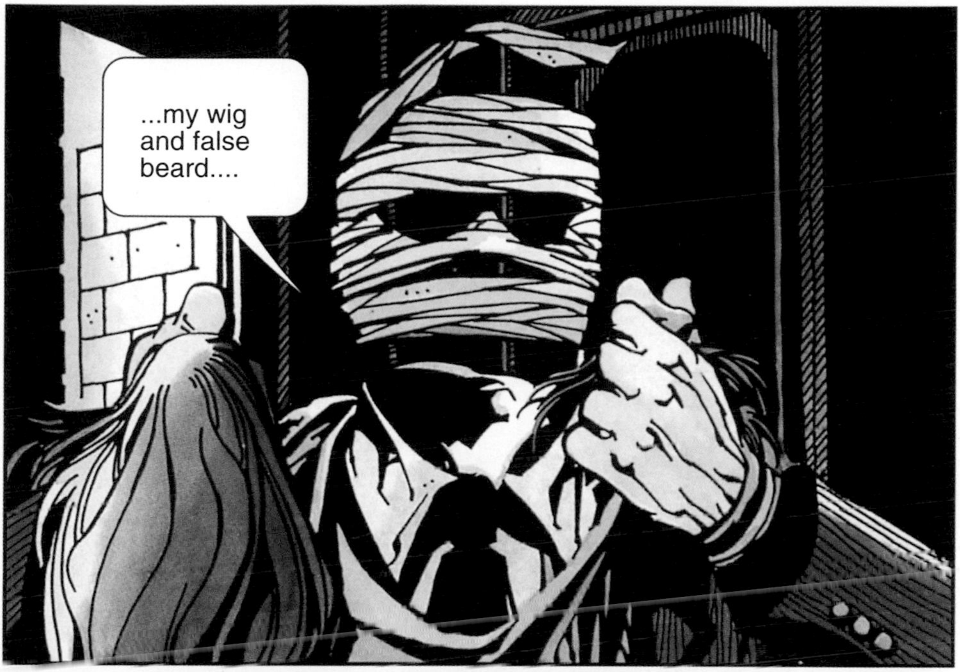
...my wig and false beard....

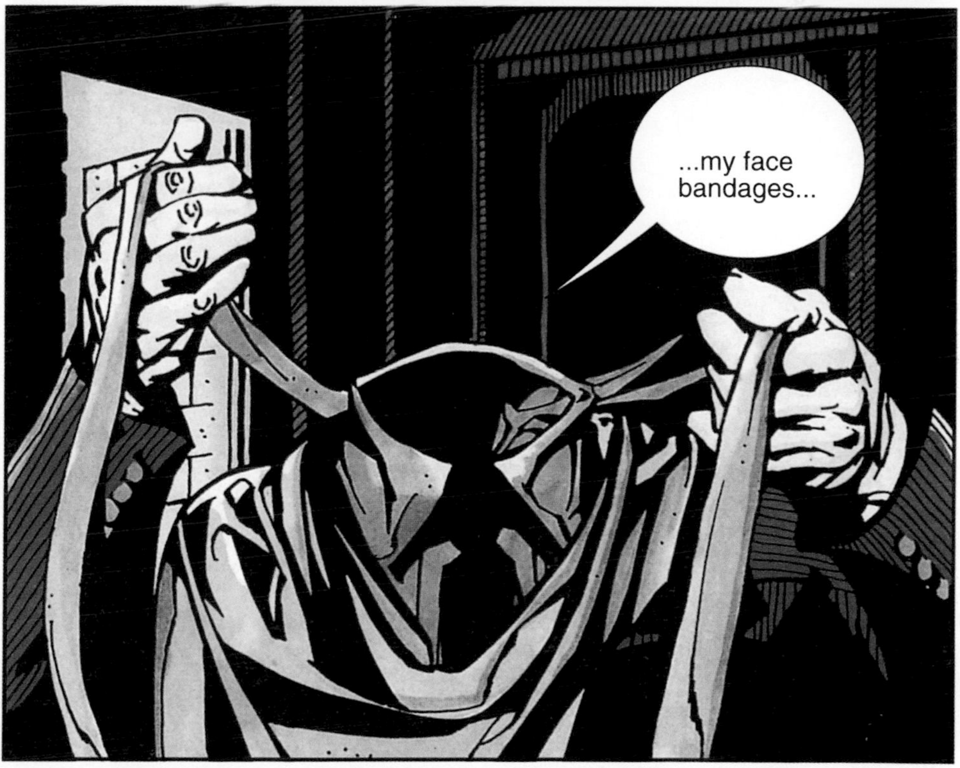
...my face bandages...

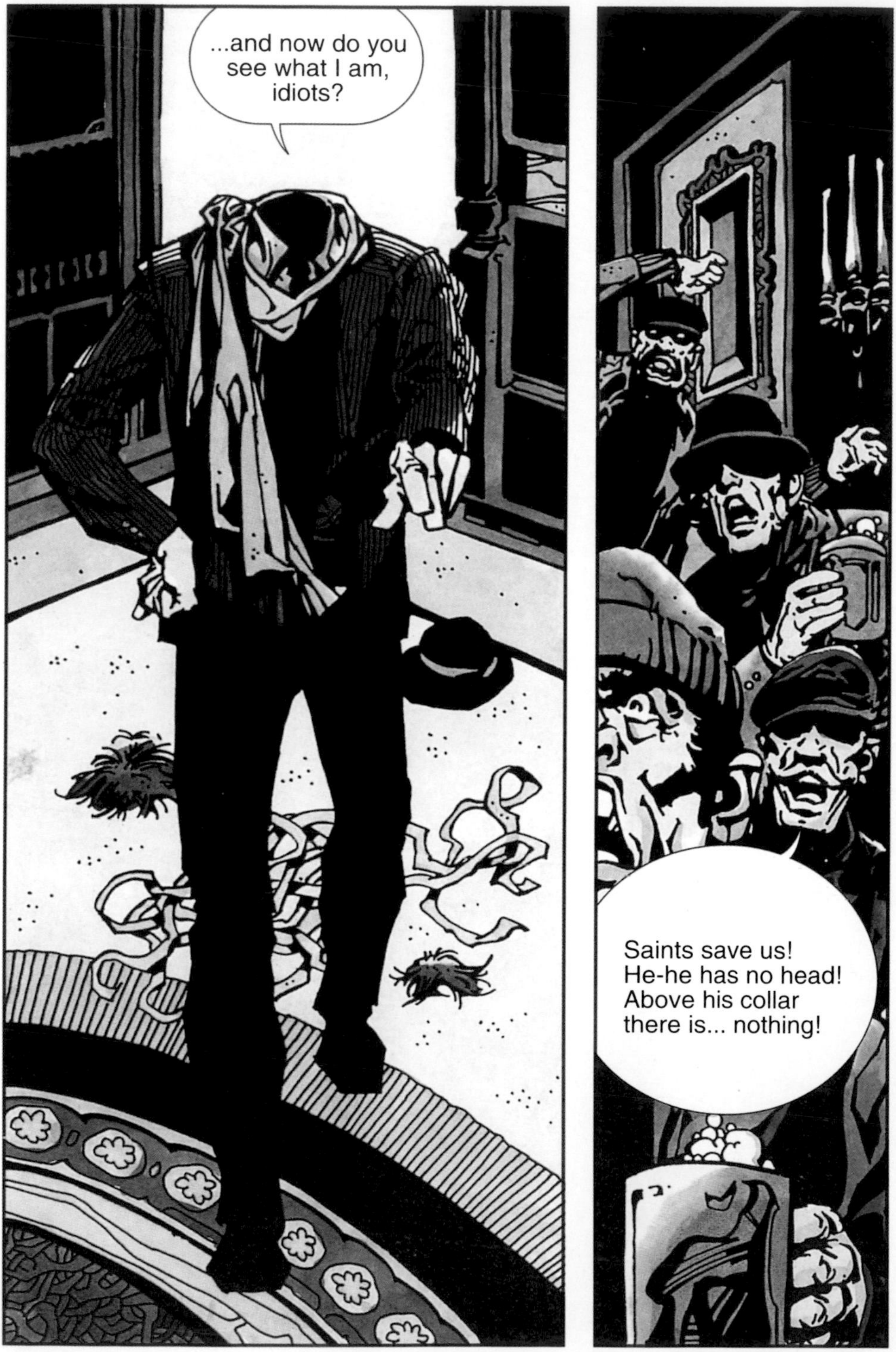
...and now do you see what I am, idiots?
Saints save us! He-he has no head! Above his collar there is... nothing!

Since she was so afraid, Mrs. Hall called the police.

Bravely, the policeman grabbed the headless man....

Do your duty, Officer Jaffers! He is a monster.

I don't see his head! Just bread and cheese!

Got you by the throat, mister!

Let go!

The Invisible Man fought, but the policeman was helped by other men....

But the Invisible Man's gloves came off during the fight, and....

Stop! I give up.

That's wise, mister. I'll put the handcuffs on you now.

Blimey! How can I handcuff a man without hands?

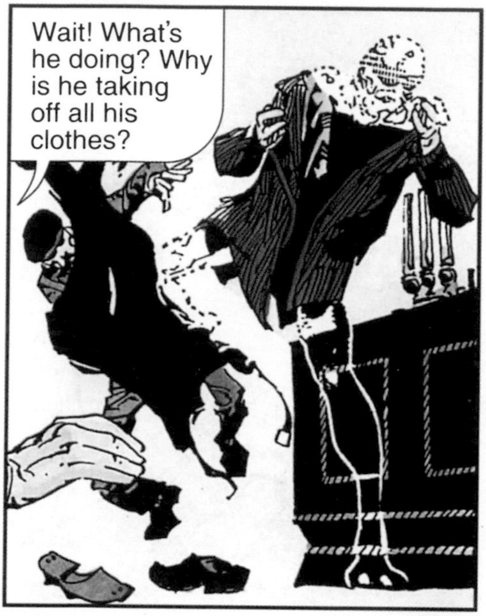
Wait! What's he doing? Why is he taking off all his clothes?

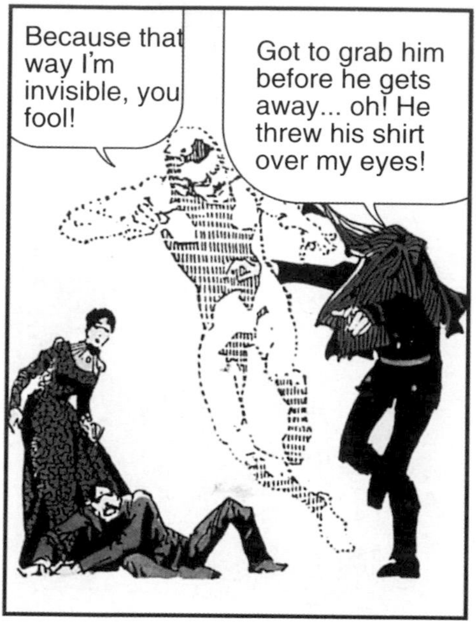
Because that way I'm invisible, you fool!
Got to grab him before he gets away... oh! He threw his shirt over my eyes!

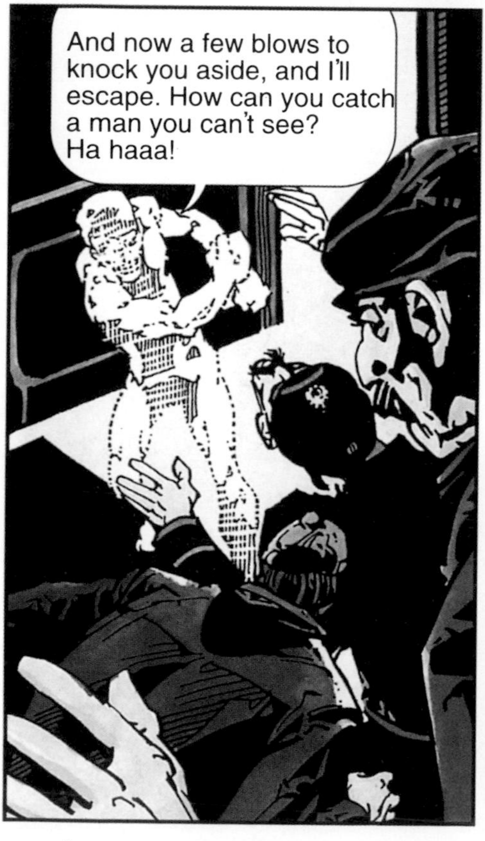
And now a few blows to knock you aside, and I'll escape. How can you catch a man you can't see? Ha haaa!

Outside....

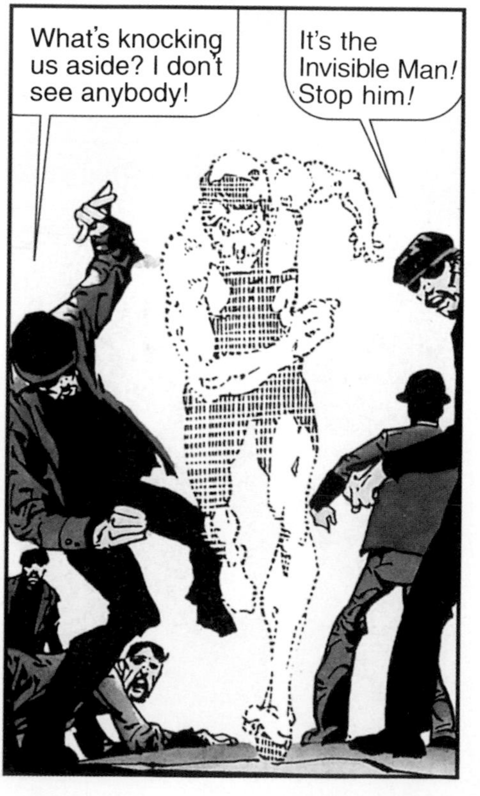
What's knocking us aside? I don't see anybody!
It's the Invisible Man! Stop him!

But they might as well have tried to stop a ghost.

And like a tornado, the unseen man rushed through the town uncaught.

Huh? No-body there at all! Am I drunk? Or seeing things?

No, you're hearing a real voice from a man you can't see. Understand?

That's silly! I'm hearing things.

Fool! Now will you believe, as two strong hands shake you like a rat? I'm right in front of you.

Don't stare and try to see me. You are simply looking through me, like thin air, I'm the invisible man.

I still can't believe it!

But one thing made the hobo believe more than anything said to him....

The voice from thin air gave orders to the shocked hobo.

Wait! Do I see bits of cheese and bread... in mid-air?

Yes, I ate some before. It won't be invisible until it's all digested.

Now that you believe in me, listen. You must help me. If you don't, I'll....

No, please. I'll do what you say!

Then you will get me clothes, food, and find me some place to stay. Brrr! I'm cold. If you help me, you'll be repaid in many ways.

I'll play along with him until I see my chance to get away.

Later, back in the village of Iping....

That invisible fellow told me to hang around here at the Coach and Horses Inn. He has some plan.

Meanwhile, in the room the Invisible Man had rented ....

Hmm! These notebooks left behind are filled with formulas.... maybe it's the secret of invisibility.

Eh? Look, the door swung open....by itself!

Quiet footsteps, and then....

Looking at the notes of a scientist is unhealthy. Now tell me, where have they put my clothes?

We don't know.

Then I need your clothes. Hand them over.

Outside, where the hobo waited....

Here, Marvel. Run away with this bundle of clothes and my three notebooks. Hurry!

I'm being chased!

Don't worry. My invisible foot trips them, see?

Meanwhile, at a fair nearby....

Vicar Bunting and I were stripped of our clothing by the Invisible Man. Watch out for him! He's dangerous.

Later, the invisible man returned to the inn.

The landlord and landlady caused me trouble all the time. I'll break every window in the place.

But later, he was sorry for the things he had done in the last hour....

I was a fool! My secret is out! Everybody will be looking for me. People will be on guard against me. What am I to do now?

Meanwhile, where Thomas Marvel, the hobo, sat on a bench in another small town nearby ...

Looky here! It tells all about an Invisible Man! What a wild story. Do you believe it?

Uh... no! It's a big joke.

The truth is, the Invisible Man is here right now, slipping stolen money into my pocket.

Hsst! keep it safe for me, Marvel.

All through town, a series of silent robberies took place.

Mommy, look! Money floating in the air!

Oh, stop your lies, Tommy. Money doesn't fly around by itself.

But meanwhile a sneaky idea came to the little hobo....

Before the Invisible Man returns for the tenth time, I'll slip away. All the money will be mine! And his notebooks too.

Some time later, a fleeing figure was seen... and heard...running toward another village.

My word! That man sounds as if his pockets are loaded with coins.

Somehow the Invisible Man trailed me. I hear his breath behind me!

The frightened hobo ran into a bar....

He's coming after me! The Invisible Man! For God's sake, help me! He said he'd kill me... and he will! Lock the door!

Open up! Open up, I say.

That's him! Don't let him in! I'll hide here behind the bar.

The next moment....

Where is he? The little crook who stole my money?

As Marvel was dragged away, one bar customer pulled a gun, and took bad aim.

You dummy! You only broke my big mirror!

When they tried to grab the unseen man ...

Out of my way, fools! Nobody can stop the Invisible Man.

In the backyard, the man with the gun fired again.

Get down, Marvel! I'll try to shoot him!

Yet, when they looked around....

That night, at the home of Dr. Kemp....

Puzzled, he went to his bedroom ...for another surprise.

Good heavens! Dr. Kemp came in before I was through taking care of my wound!

Who's here?

A blood-stained bandage! How can it hang in mid-air?

Keep your nerve, Kemp. I'm the Invisible Man you read about in the papers.

Bah! I don't believe in such tales. I'll reach out but I won't feel anything solid.... Heavens! A real hand!

Steady, Kemp, for God's sake! I need your help badly. Steady!

When the doctor tried to shout for help....

That will keep you from yelling. Now listen. I'm no supernatural creature. You know me... I'm Griffin of University College, where you were also a student years ago.

The gag was removed when the doctor quieted down....

Griffin? Yes, I remember. Six feet tall... broad shoulders. And you won the medal for chemistry.

The doctor gave him a robe . . . .

That's better. But I'm starving too.

I'll bring you something.

But what deviltry could make you invisible to the eye?

No deviltry, Kemp. It's simply a drug I've taken. But the cold air outside almost froze me... brrrrr! I need clothing.

Shortly....

Ah, delicious!

But something puzzles me. If you're invisible, why is your blood visible!

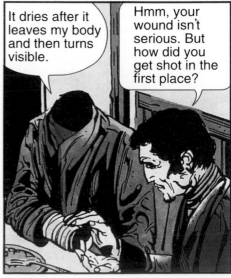

It dries after it leaves my body and then turns visible.

Hmm, your wound isn't serious. But how did you get shot in the first place?

My helper, Marvel, turned me in and tried to make off with money I gave him. When I chased him to a bar, a man shot at me. But forget that. I'll have a cigar now.

It was a strange sight to Dr. Kemp....

Nothing like a good smoke after eating.

How odd! I can see the smoke going into your mouth and throat and down into your lungs as you inhale.

But the money you gave the hobo... where did you get it?

None of your business, Kemp! Right now I'm very tired. I haven't slept for three days and nights.

Help yourself to my bed. Why haven't you slept before?

Because I'm afraid that if I go to sleep, somebody might find me, and I'd be caught.

Oh, what a fool I am! Hope I haven't put that idea into your head, Kemp!

Uh... I give you my word I won't turn you in.

Then I can sleep soundly. Good night, Kemp.

He locked the door. He's taking no chances.

Dr. Kemp stayed up, reading the newspaper stories about his strange guest.

Good heavens! The man is insane. He's a crazy killer.

TERROR STORY FROM IPING!

WHOLE TOWN IN SUSSEX PANICS!

INVISIBLE MAN STRIKES!

The doctor stayed up till dawn, trying to decide what to do.

He may do even more horrible things. And he's in my house. What should I do about him? Should I keep my promise not to tell anyone?

No! A promise to a crazy man means nothing. I'll write to Colonel Adye of the Port Burdock police, and tell him to come and capture this invisible man!

A crash sounded upstairs and after the door was unlocked....

What happened, Griffin?

My sore arm pained me as I washed. Had a fit of temper and smashed the bowl. It's nothing.

After Kemp led his unseen guest to the breakfast room.

I want you to be my partner, Kemp. We can do big things together. An invisible man is a man of power!

Before I can promise anything, I must know all about this invisibility of yours.

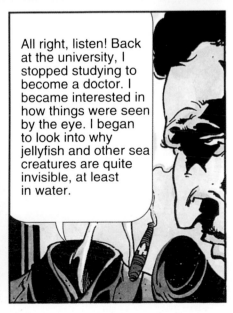

All right, listen! Back at the university, I stopped studying to become a doctor. I became interested in how things were seen by the eye. I began to look into why jellyfish and other sea creatures are quite invisible, at least in water.

The question was, could things be made invisible in air, not water? My studies showed me that besides the coloring of skin and hair and the redness of blood, a man's body cells could easily be made transparent.

And then you found out how to turn even skin, hair, and blood colorless?

Exactly! A chemical mixture could do it, along with the rays from two small dynamos run by a gas engine. I first tested out my plan on a cat and....

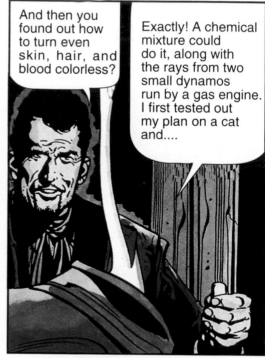

....after it drank the drug, the dynamo rays turned it as invisible as thin air!

It worked! Now I can try it on myself and become the Invisible Man!

It worked slowly. First my skin turned pure white...
then my whole body became milky, like cloudy
glass... then my body began disappearing except
for hair, fingernails, and bones.

Finally, as the dynamo rays kept working on my body....

No picture in my mirror! Nothing! The Invisible Man is born!

But the landlord and his two husky step-sons suddenly came in, because of the noise of the dynamos . . . .

What's going on in here? Make him tell...huh?

Nobody here!

When they went out, wondering, I slipped out with my three notebooks containing the invisibility formulas and....

I'll mail them to myself at General Delivery at the Great Portland Street Station. I can pick them up later.

Then I sneaked back into my room and piled up scraps of paper....

The rest of my chemicals and apparatus I can burn up.

Of course the whole house burned down... but I had to do it, Kemp, to protect my secret!

He was a madman then already. He didn't care about people's lives or property!

At first, I felt happy when I walked away...

I feel like a man with good eyes in a city of blind people. I can see them, but they can't see me!

But I didn't think about what would happen if others could not see me!

Oops! What did I bump into? I see nothing!

More trouble as I crossed a street....

But that gave me a clever idea!

But it was a cold day in January and in my bare skin, I was very cold, so then....

But later, when a woman stopped the cab....

Another danger I had not seen was that dogs have very sharp noses...

Worst of all, two boys with sharp eyes noticed something peculiar....

Looky! Muddy footprints made by bare feet! Let's follow them.

Those brats made me run into a yard and painfully climb over a wall.

Who is making these bare footprints? After him!

Those boys told others, and a whole bunch of people are after me, including policemen! How can I escape?

I stopped and....

The sun dried the street ahead. If I wipe off this mud, my tracks won't show anymore.

Though not being chased anymore, I had plenty of small troubles.

My feet are sore... My back aches... I've got sores where people bumped me ... and I'm getting a bad cold! Well, at least I'm safe from being followed again.

I left behind some very puzzled people!

The footprints ended suddenly, right here! Where did he go? And why was he walking around barefoot, in winter?

Must be out of his head!

But then, to my horror....

An idea flashed into my mind.

And soon, I was happy and warm on a pile of mattresses.

When closing time came, I woke up and...

When the cleaning people are done, I'll wander around and find what I want.

...and I'm all dressed up!

At last...

The place is all locked up and I'm alone. Now to visit a half-dozen different departments...

But I may as well sleep the rest of the night. I'll keep my clothes on for an early start tomorrow, leaving the store.

But I overslept and suddenly sat up to find the store full of clerks!

That man! He has no face!

That does it! Now everybody will chase me.

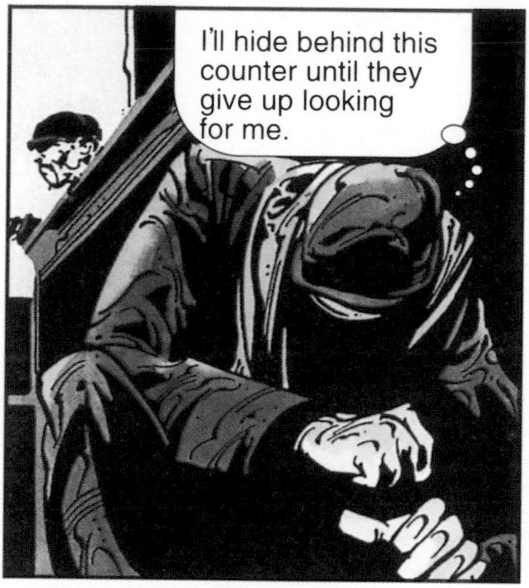
I'll hide behind this counter until they give up looking for me.

But I was found too soon...

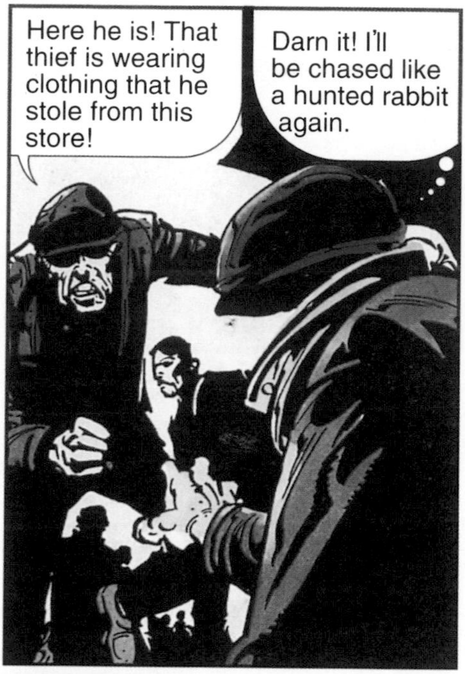
Here he is! That thief is wearing clothing that he stole from this store!
Darn it! I'll be chased like a hunted rabbit again.

Oddly enough, I did not think to take off my clothes and easily escape as the Invisible Man!

I fought my way through different departments...

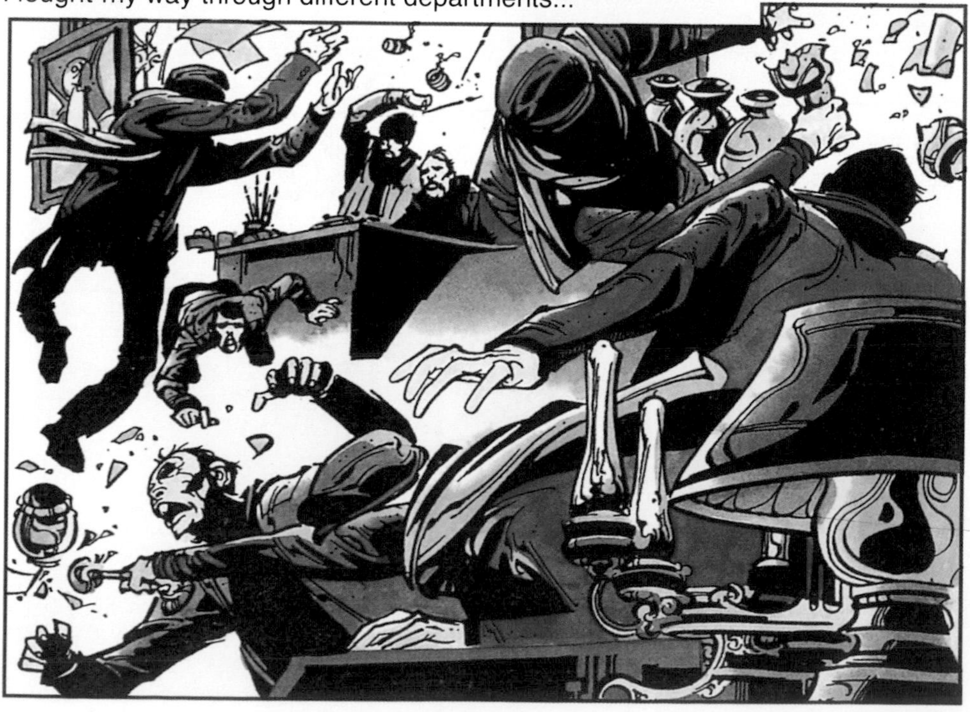

...and finally had time to rest.

I should have done this in the first place... take off my clothes and become invisible!

The hunting party is here, but too late to stop me.

Look! Something flying through the air! The thief must have run behind something. Find him!

They looked everywhere but where I was.

As the store became busier, I left it the same way I had entered ...unclothed.

While they waste their time looking for me, I'll have breakfast... without paying.

That plan failed. Anyway, the snow stopped and the sun is out, drying the sidewalks so I can walk around freely. But what shall I do next?

As Griffin continued his amazing tale to Dr. Kemp....

At that moment, I sadly came to know that being invisible was not all good; it had many things against it! With bare skin I was freezing... yet wearing clothes made me ugly without a face... if I ate too much the undigested food would give me away... dogs could smell me with their noses... snow would show my footprints.

What was worse, I could see how rain would show my human form... fog would turn me into a visible ghost... even dust and soot falling on my skin would make me visible again.

But finally, another answer to my problem came to me...

I can dress up if I cover my invisible head and face with a wig and false beard! I'll get them in this shop, and clothes too.

The shopkeeper had heard the bell door tinkle, but when he came out...

But I had to stay still when the shopkeeper returned to his lunch.

The next time he left to serve a customer ....

But while I was looking through some old clothes...

But he knew some-
thing was wrong.....

He's locking every
door! That will stop
me from looking for
the things I need.

I'll have to knock
him out and take
his keys.

There, old man!
That'll keep you
quiet while I
finish looking around.

After choosing some old clothes, I found other things I needed.

A wig... black beard.
dark glasses...and a
mask! Now I can go
out among other
people safely.

But I need money too. I'll take the old man's collection of gold coins.

But my new disguise led to another problem...

I can't eat unless I remove my mask and that would show my invisible face! I'm starving... yet I can't touch that food!

I went to another place and ordered a private room....

At last I can feed myself!

Later, I went to the Great Portland Street Post Office and claimed my package...

With my notes I'll experiment and find a way to become visible again. Being invisible all the time has too many problems. I'll rent a room in some small town and buy chemicals with the stolen money.

As Griffin's strange story ended....

So that was how I came to Iping and the Coach and Horses Inn. But it was a mistake to get that hobo, Thomas Marvel, to help me. He not only took money from me, but also hid my three notebooks. Now I need a new partner...

...you, Kemp! With your help I can take over town after town! To begin with, I'll kill anybody who gets in my way until I run this town. Are you with me?

He'll want to kill to get power! What shall I say?

But Dr. Kemp was saved from answering when....

Wait! I hear footsteps coming upstairs!

Nonsense! It's your imagination.

But I hope it's Colonel Adye!

You tricked me! It's the police, isn't it? I'll toss off my robe and slip away as the Invisible Man.

No, you won't! I'll lock you in here!

But as luck would have it....

As the two men fought, the door opened six inches...

Kemp was flung back...

Climbing the stairs, Colonel Adye was pushed out of the way....

When Dr. Kemp had recovered...

After the doctor explained it all....

My God! The Invisible Man got away!

Tell me the whole story, Kemp.

...and so, the Invisible Man plans to kill and injure people to get power! Colonel, you must stop him from leaving this town.

I'll have men guard the railroad stations and all roads. We'll get him.

The whole countryside joined the police in guarding every way of escape...

That Invisible Man won't get past us!

Even if we don't see him, our dogs will pick up his smell!

One poor man met the Invisible Man...

It does no good killing this man. I can't break through those lines of waiting men.

Back in town, the Invisible Man understood he was trapped....

Dr. Kemp caused all this. I'll get him.

WANTED

The Invisible Man! By order of the police, railroad trains have been stopped.... roads closed.... no coaches to leave... keep all doors and windows locked....

Kemp found a note under his door....

I AM THE TERROR! I ANNOUNCE THE EPOCH OF THE INVISIBLE MAN! I WILL SLAY ALL IN MY WAY. AND DEATH WILL COME FIRST TO THAT TRAITOR... DR. KEMP

That's right. Close all shutters and lock the doors. Then take this note to Colonel Adye. I'll be safe here.

Some time later.....

Colonel Adye! Why did you come here? Didn't you read the note I sent by my maid?

The maid says the Invisible Man grabbed the note from her. What was in it, Kemp?

I planned a trap for the Invisible Man....which he has now read! That spoils my plan.

Then the next move is up to him.

And it came with a loud noise....

That madman Griffin is breaking all your upstairs windows!

It won't do him any good! He can't climb up here.

Colonel Adye decided to go to the police station for help, but....

Stop, Colonel! Go back to the house!

The Invisible Man! But you won't stop, me, sir, I'll shoot....

Colonel Adye tried one more trick....

Dr. Kemp was really afraid....

Soon in the kitchen....

Shortly after, Kemp let in his maid and two policemen she brought back....

But that door was chopped down too, and then....

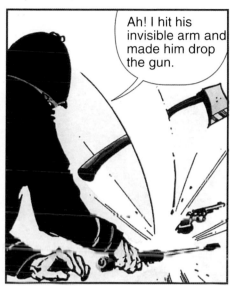

As the brave policeman swung again at his invisible enemy....

But the other policeman grabbed up the poker....

When the policeman looked for Dr. Kemp....

When Dr. Kemp ran to a neighbor's house for help....

The doctor tried any trick to slow down the killer.

Further on....

But one of the workman threw his shovel through the air...

But the Invisible Man's fighting suddenly stopped and a strange sight met their wondering eyes.

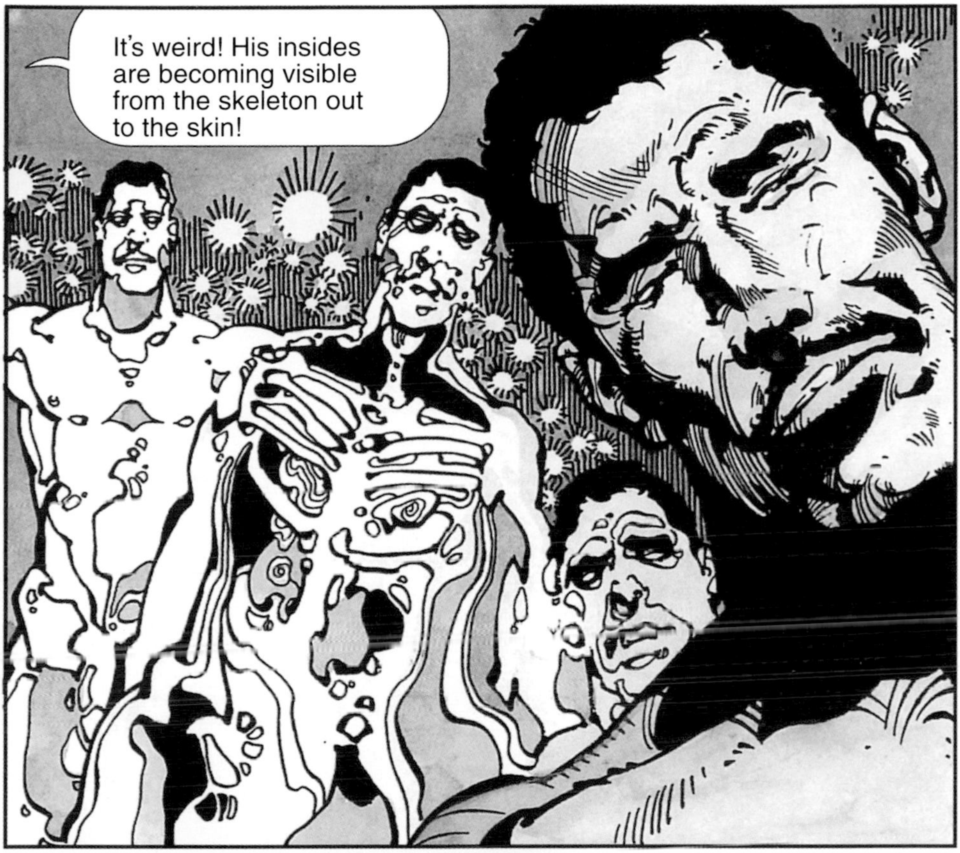
It's weird! His insides are becoming visible from the skeleton out to the skin!

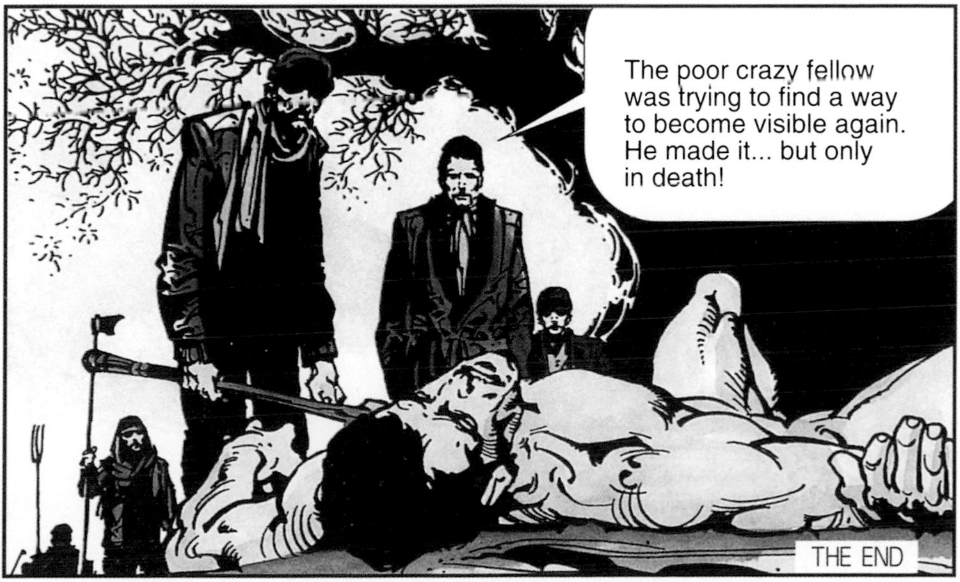
The poor crazy fellow was trying to find a way to become visible again. He made it... but only in death!
THE END